Half and Half

By JoAnne Nelson • Pictures by Noelle Giddings

MODERN CURRICULUM PRESS

PROJECT DIRECTOR: Judith E. Nayer
COVER DESIGN: Elaine A. Groth

Published by Modern Curriculum Press

Modern Curriculum Press, Inc.
A division of Simon & Schuster
13900 Prospect Road, Cleveland, Ohio 44136

ISBN 0-8136-4315-5 (STY PK)   ISBN 0-8136-4311-2 (BK)

10 9 8 7 6 5 4 3   94 93 92

Adrian Sly was a pie maker.
One day she made sixteen apple pies,
and left them on the counter to cool.

Soon a peddler came by and saw the pies.
"My, my," said the peddler.
"What nice pies you have!
  May I buy half of them?"

"Why, yes," said Adrian Sly,
as she counted out half of the pies.

The peddler loaded the pies in his cart
and went off down the road to the market.

On the way to the market
the peddler came to a fork in the road.
There he met a group of travelers.

"My, my," said the travelers.
"What nice pies you have!
May we buy half of them?"

"Why, yes," said the peddler,
  as he counted out half of the pies.

The travelers put the pies in their packs
  and went up the road to the mountains.

The peddler continued on his way to the market.
Soon he came to a cobbler's shop.

"My, my," said the cobbler and his wife.
"What nice pies you have!
 Will you trade half of your pies
 for a new pair of shoes?"

"Why, yes," said the peddler,
looking at his worn-out shoes.
So he counted out half of the pies.

The peddler put on his new shoes
and went on down the road.

Soon the peddler came to a lake.
He was feeling VERY tired, and VERY hungry.

"My, my," said the peddler.
"These ARE nice pies!
I think I'll have half of them myself."

So the peddler left his cart
and sat down beside the lake to eat the pie.
Soon he fell fast asleep in the sun.

While the peddler was asleep,
the cart started to roll down the hill.
It rolled down the road and past the lake.

The cart rolled on and on—
    past the cobbler's shop,
    past the fork in the road,
    and right up to the door of the pie shop.

"My, my," said the pie man.
"What a nice pie!
I think I'll take half
of this pie home with me."

So he cut the pie in half,
and left the other half on the counter.

Just then Adrian Sly came out
from the back of the shop.
She noticed the pie on the counter.

"My, my," said Adrian Sly.
"What a nice piece of pie!
I think I'll have half."

So she cut the piece in half,
and then she ate it.

"My, my," said Adrian Sly.
"This tastes just like MY apple pie!"

AND SHE ATE IT ALL UP.